by Elizabeth Catanese illustrated by Benedetta Capriotti

MT. OLYMPUS THEME PARK

THE HUNTING HOUSE

Shakespeare's Sonnets

Poems

An Imprint of Magic Wagon
abdobooks.com

With gratitude to my parents, Paul and Mary Carol Catanese, whose love for each other is "an ever-fixed mark." -EC

To Giulia and Matteo. -BC

abdobooks.com

Published by Magic Wagon, a division of ABDO, PO Box 398166, Minneapolis, Minnesota 55439.

Printed in the United States of America, North Mankato, Minnesota.
052021
092021

Written by Elizabeth Catanese
Illustrated by Benedetta Capriotti
Edited by Bridget O'Brien
Art Directed by Laura Graphenteen

Library of Congress Control Number: 2020948147

Publisher's Cataloging-in-Publication Data

Names: Catanese, Elizabeth, author. | Capriotti, Benedetta, illustrator.
Title: The hunting house / by Elizabeth Catanese ; illustrated by Benedetta Capriotti.
Description: Minneapolis, Minnesota : Magic Wagon, 2022. | Series: Mt. Olympus theme park
Summary: Miles wants to focus on archery instead of school during a trip to Mt. Olympus Theme Park with his dad, but when he opens a secret door to the myth of Aphrodite and Adonis, Miles has to use one of his teacher's lessons to help the hunter.
Identifiers: ISBN 9781098230371 (lib. bdg.) | ISBN 9781098230937 (ebook) | ISBN 9781098231217 (Read-to-Me ebook)
Subjects: LCSH: Amusement parks--Juvenile fiction. | Mythology, Greek--Juvenile fiction. | Archery--Juvenile fiction. | Divine beings--Juvenile fiction. | Amusement rides--Juvenile fiction. | Gods, Greek--Juvenile fiction
Classification: DDC [FIC]--dc23

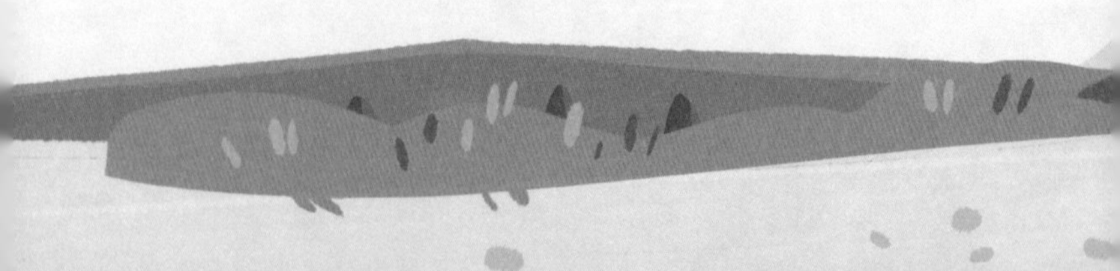

Table of Contents

Chapter 1

A BONFIRE

CRACKLE. Flames leap into the air during Miles's end-of-school bonfire. This year Miles is not only BURNING branches but also his English tests.

William Shakespeare
Sonnets

Miles's English teacher, Mr. Daniels, decided to TEACH Shakespeare's sonnets for three WHOLE months. Sonnets are fourteen-line poems written in hard-to-understand English. *And* they are often about love. What could be worse?

Thank goodness it's time for summer: archery, theme parks, and months with his dad and his dad's girlfriend Kate, in New Jersey.

"Hey, kiddo," says Miles's dad, JOINING him outside. "Do you want to go to Mt. Olympus Theme Park tomorrow to CELEBRATE the end of school?" They love going to the park based on ancient Greek myths.

“Yes! Let’s go to the Aphrodite’s FRIGHTIES part first,” Miles exclaims. “I’ll bet I can **unlock** the door in the Hunting House ride this time.”

The indoor roller coaster has a challenge. If you shoot *all* the **mythological** creatures with your electronic longbow, a door will take you right into the myth of Adonis and Aphrodite. No one has **EVER** done it!

"Well, I think that ride is rigged," says Miles's dad, "but if anyone can unlock the door to a myth, it's you!"

On the drive to Mt. Olympus Theme Park, Miles and his dad usually talk about FUN things, like archery. Miles is surprised when his dad wants to talk about his D in English.

"I HATE English," says Miles. "Mom already told me I need to do better next year."

"How about if we get you a TUTOR?" asks his dad. "Grades matter."

"I thought you were BAD at English too," says Miles.

"I just want you to be better than me," his dad says. Miles doesn't understand. His dad is the **best** person he knows.

With the gates of the theme park in sight, Miles and his dad **STOP** at a red light. A deer appears. And it **STICKS** its head right in Miles's open window!

Chapter 11
OH DEER!

"Hello," the deer says. Miles **gasps**. He has never met a talking deer.

"I'm Artemis, goddess of the hunt. I'm your **GUIDE** to the Hunting House. See you at the park," the deer says, ***RUNNING*** off.

“Mt. Olympus is taking things a bit too FAR,” says Miles’s dad. “All characters should STAY in the park!” They LAUGH as they pull into the parking lot.

Artemis, who now **LOOKS** more like a person than a deer, **GREETS** Miles and his dad at the gate of Mt. Olympus.

"Would you like some COUPONS for free candy apples?" she asks Miles's dad.

"It's our lucky day." He takes a wad of pink coupons from Artemis.

Miles's dad leaves to get candy apples while Miles goes to the Hunting House with Artemis.

ARTEMIS

"I've got an IMPORTANT strategy to tell you about," says Artemis. "As you know, no one has been successful in unlocking the door to the myth before and we need your HELP. To hit the last creature and open the door, you have to shoot behind you. Can you do that?"

"Absolutely!" Miles EXCLAIMS as they arrive.

THE HUNTING HOUSE

Artemis hands Miles his electronic longbow, then **STRAPS** him into the roller-coaster car. "Best of luck," Artemis says.

Throughout the ride, Miles hits all of the targets from the **GLOWING** green centaurs and the manticores, to the three griffins and the Gorgons. He even hits a cyclops in its one eye!

He sees
the Chimera
and knows the
MOMENT is here. Miles
trusts what Artemis said
and SHOOTS behind him.

Suddenly, Miles is FLYING from the roller coaster. In front of him is a door.

Maybe, just maybe, he has unlocked the door to the myth. The only problem is the door is closed. And he is about to CRASH into it!

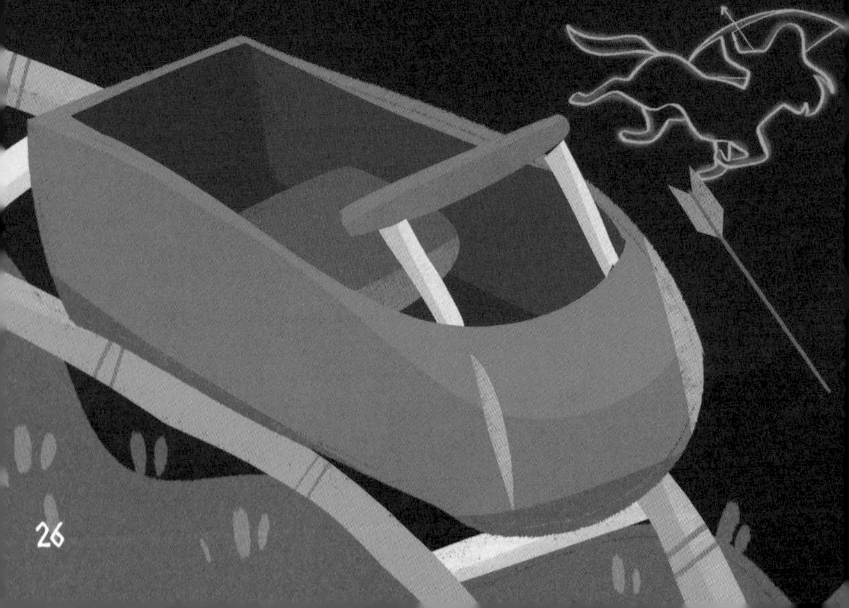

Chapter III

IMPRESSING A GIRLFRIEND

Miles OPENS his eyes. He's in a forest. His longbow and a pile of ARROWS are next to him. The door must have opened after all. *I did it,* he thinks.

Miles walks through the forest. *What happens next?* he WONDERS.

Out of nowhere, a giant boar CHARGES at him. Miles grabs his longbow and shoots. A narrow miss! The SCARED boar runs away. But now something else is charging at him. Another ANIMAL?

No. It's a muscular guy with brown wavy hair and a white toga. "Oh no! I was going to KILL that boar! You scared it away!"

"Ummm. SORRY. I'm Miles. And you are?"

The man ignores him. "Now I can't IMPRESS Aphrodite."

"Are you Adonis?" Miles asks. He must have opened the secret door.

"Yes," says Adonis. "You have to help me find another boar to slay to IMPRESS my girlfriend."

Miles remembers the myth of Aphrodite and Adonis. Actually, Aphrodite, the goddess of love and beauty, got mad at Adonis for KILLING creatures. It didn't impress her at all!

"I HATE to break it to you," says Miles, "but your girlfriend is going to be mad if you KILL a boar. How about if we find another way to IMPRESS her?"

"Why should I believe you?" Adonis asks.

"Artemis, goddess of the hunt, **SENT** me." Miles doesn't mention the park.

Adonis's eyes widen. "I'd **love** your help."

Chapter IV
A SHAKESPEAREAN WIN

"Tell me some things Aphrodite likes," says Miles.

"No IDEA," says Adonis.

"But isn't she your girlfriend?" asks Miles.

Adonis frowns. "She often reads this book of poems. Love poems. She goes on about something called sonnets," Adonis says excitedly.

I'm the **wrong** *kid for this job,*

thinks Miles. He can't REMEMBER a single thing from the sonnet unit in English class this year.

Except . . . something comes back. Shakespeare's Sonnet 116 has a line about how love is "an ever-fixed mark."

Shakespeare's saying that love is as stable *as an archery target*, Mr. Daniels had said. He knew that Miles would connect to archery.

Miles knows what to do. "I'm going to HELP you learn Shakespeare's Sonnet 116. When you're done, you can tell Aphrodite you love her more than hunting."

For the rest of the afternoon, Miles helps Adonis memorize the lines. He goes with the hunter when he recites them to Aphrodite, a short woman with blond curls and a pink dress.

"I love you, Adonis."

Aphrodite twirls happily

in her dress. She gives him a kiss.

"This kid HELPED me." Adonis beams. "Is there anything I can do for you in return?"

"Can you help me get back to my dad? He's probably EATING all the candy apples."

"I don't know what a CANDY apple is," says Adonis, "but I know where there's a door that MIGHT take you back."

A door in front of a tree pulls Miles through. It **plops** him next to his dad in the theme park.

"I did it," says Miles. "I went into the myth."

"Will you get a prize for that?" his dad asks.

"I don't think so," says Miles. "But guess how I HELPED Adonis IMPRESS his girlfriend?! By teaching him a Shakespearean sonnet!"

"WOW!" says Miles's dad. "Kate loves poetry. Can you teach me those lines too, kiddo?"

"Only if you SHARE that candy apple," Miles declares.